P9-CRW-733

Saline District Library

3 4604 91004 5821

j Cho v.103
Montgomery, Ramsey.

Grave robbers

WITHDRAWN

"Choose Your Own Adventure is the best thing that has come along since books themselves."
—Alysha Beyer, age 11

"I didn't read much before, but now I read my Choose Your Own Adventure books almost every night."
—Chris Brogan, age 13

"I love the control I have over what happens next."
—Kosta Efstathiou, age 17

"Choose Your Own Adventure books are so much fun to read and collect—I want them all!"
—Brendan Davin, age 11

And teachers like this series, too:
"We have read and reread, worn thin, loved, loaned, bought for others, and donated to school libraries our Choose Your Own Adventure books."

CHOOSE YOUR OWN ADVENTURE®—
AND MAKE READING MORE FUN!

Bantam Books in the Choose Your Own Adventure® series
Ask your bookseller for the books you have missed

#1 THE CAVE OF TIME
#2 JOURNEY UNDER THE SEA
#3 DANGER IN THE DESERT
#4 SPACE AND BEYOND
#5 THE CURSE OF THE
    HAUNTED MANSION
#6 SPY TRAP
#7 MESSAGE FROM SPACE
#8 DEADWOOD CITY
#9 WHO KILLED HARLOWE
    THROMBEY?
#10 THE LOST JEWELS
#22 SPACE PATROL
#31 VAMPIRE EXPRESS
#52 GHOST HUNTER
#53 THE CASE OF THE SILK
    KING
#66 SECRET OF THE NINJA
#71 SPACE VAMPIRE
#73 BEYOND THE GREAT WALL
#74 LONGHORN TERRITORY
#75 PLANET OF THE DRAGONS
#76 THE MONA LISA IS MISSING!
#77 THE FIRST OLYMPICS
#78 RETURN TO ATLANTIS
#79 MYSTERY OF THE SACRED
    STONES

#80 THE PERFECT PLANET
#81 TERROR IN AUSTRALIA
#82 HURRICANE!
#83 TRACK OF THE BEAR
#84 YOU ARE A MONSTER
#85 INCA GOLD
#86 KNIGHTS OF THE ROUND TABLE
#87 EXILED TO EARTH
#88 MASTER OF KUNG FU
#89 SOUTH POLE SABOTAGE
#90 MUTINY IN SPACE
#91 YOU ARE A SUPERSTAR
#92 RETURN OF THE NINJA
#93 CAPTIVE!
#94 BLOOD ON THE HANDLE
#95 YOU ARE A GENIUS
#96 STOCK CAR CHAMPION
#97 THROUGH THE BLACK HOLE
#98 YOU ARE A MILLIONAIRE
#99 REVENGE OF THE RUSSIAN
    GHOST
#100 THE WORST DAY OF YOUR LIFE
#101 ALIEN, GO HOME!
#102 MASTER OF TAE KWON DO
#103 GRAVE ROBBERS

#1 JOURNEY TO THE YEAR 3000 (A Choose Your Own Adventure Super Adventure)
#2 DANGER ZONES (A Choose Your Own Adventure Super Adventure)

GRAVE ROBBERS

BY RAMSEY MONTGOMERY

ILLUSTRATED BY LESLIE MORRILL

An R.A. Montgomery Book

SALINE DISTRICT LIBRARY
555 N. Maple Road
Saline, MI 48176

BANTAM BOOKS
NEW YORK • TORONTO • LONDON • SYDNEY • AUCKLAND

RL 4, age 10 and up

GRAVE ROBBERS
A Bantam Book / July 1990

*CHOOSE YOUR OWN ADVENTURE® is a registered trademark of
Bantam Books, a division of Bantam Doubleday Dell Publishing Group,
Inc. Registered in U.S. Patent and Trademark Office and elsewhere.*

Original conception of Edward Packard

*Cover art by Romas Kukalis.
Interior illustrations by Leslie Morrill.*

*All rights reserved.
Copyright © 1990 by Ramsey Montgomery.
Cover art and interior illustrations copyright © 1990 by Bantam Books.
No part of this book may be reproduced or transmitted
in any form or by any means, electronic or mechanical,
including photocopying, recording, or by any information
storage and retrieval system, without permission in writing from
the publisher.
For information address: Bantam Books.*

ISBN 0-553-28554-8

Published simultaneously in the United States and Canada

*Bantam Books are published by Bantam Books, a division of Bantam Double-
day Dell Publishing Group, Inc. Its trademark, consisting of the words
"Bantam Books" and the portrayal of a rooster, is Registered in U.S. Patent
and Trademark Office and in other countries. Marca Registrada. Bantam
Books, 666 Fifth Avenue, New York, New York 10103.*

PRINTED IN THE UNITED STATES OF AMERICA

OPM   0 9 8 7 6 5 4 3 2 1

To Olga Montgomery

WARNING!!!

Do not read this book straight through from beginning to end. These pages contain many different adventures that you may have when you attempt to stop the destruction of the ancient Anasazi Indian burial grounds. From time to time as you read along, you will be asked to make a choice. Your choice may lead to success or disaster!

The adventures you have are the results of your choices. You are responsible because you choose! After you make a choice, follow the instructions to see what happens to you next.

Think carefully before you make a decision. The Southwest could be fun, but whoever is robbing the graves for the valuable pottery could be dangerous. Even if you do return the stolen artifacts to their proper grave sites, you may not necessarily make it home!

Good luck!

You stare at your television set as the following special report is announced:

"*. . . State, local, and tribal police remain mystified by the recent theft and destruction of the Anasazi Indian sites. There are literally thousands of these ancient ruins throughout the canyonlands of Arizona, New Mexico, and Nevada, and thieves have brazenly robbed some of the best-known Anasazi ruins—right under the noses of the law!*

"*Vandals' theft of the valuable pottery and wanton destruction of these sites has left investigators angered. In their haste to locate these priceless artifacts, thieves have used pickaxes, shovels, even backhoes, destroying the ruins in the process.*

"*As you can see, the Anasazi built their homes to blend in with the landscape. Made of stone and mud bricks, these dwellings became a part of canyon walls and cliffs; the Anasazi way of life was in harmony with nature until hundreds of years ago, when they mysteriously vanished.*"

You can hardly believe it. Your interest in the Anasazi started last year when you spent the summer with your great-aunt, who lives in New Mexico. She introduced you to the Anasazi. She also introduced you to Daniel Chinaua and his son Edward "Running Coyote." You and Edward quickly became close friends. Your friendship was strengthened by your interest in the Anasazi Indians. The two of you vowed to try and solve the mystery of their disappearance together.

Turn to page 2.

The television reporter continues the special report by showing different types of pottery that the Anasazi made.

"This might look insignificant to many of our viewers, but pottery and other artifacts like this give us history and insights into the Indian culture. Anthropologists and historians believe that secrets locked up in the ancient existence of this civilization could benefit us all. They might even serve as warnings to us today, warnings that could help prevent our modern civilization from disappearing just as the Anasazi did hundreds of years ago."

Nodding your head in agreement, you feel an overpowering urge to stop the destruction of the sites and to uncover the secrets of the Anasazi.

"With us here tonight is the chief of the Navaho tribal police, Daniel Chinaua," the report continues. *"Mr. Chinaua, what can you tell us about the Anasazi?"*

You don't wait to hear what the chief says; you know it already from your long days hiking the canyons with him and his son Edward. You reach for the phone and anxiously await the ring at the other end of the line, some eighteen hundred miles away.

"Ed? It's me. I've just seen your dad on TV. Is it really as bad as it seems? I mean the gang who's busting up the sites. Is the damage really as severe as they say?"

Go on to the next page.

"I'm sure glad you called," Edward says. "I was just going to call you. Can you come out here and help us? If you can catch the next plane to Albuquerque, I'll explain everything then."

It's summer vacation. You've got money saved up from your part-time job at the gas station in town, and just last week your parents even suggested that it might be a good time for you to go back to New Mexico.

"I'll see you in Albuquerque tomorrow afternoon, Ed. I'm on my way!"

A flight leaves early the next morning, and you're able to get a reservation. It doesn't take you long to pack. Your clothes, books, and rock-climbing and camping gear fit into two blue canvas duffels. The next morning your parents drop you off, and before long you're in the air.

Edward meets you at the airport. It is really good to see him again after almost a whole year. Once the two of you are in his Jeep and headed out of town, you ask, "What's going on?"

"Thieves are destroying the ruins! They've taken all of the valuable pottery and are selling it on the black market. Anasazi pots sell for thousands of dollars. They're in huge demand. Private collectors value them highly, and they don't care how they get them. They just want to show the pottery off to their friends."

"The reports say that there aren't any clues. What can we do? We have to stop these thieves!" You surprise yourself with the determination in your voice and your anger.

Turn to page 89.

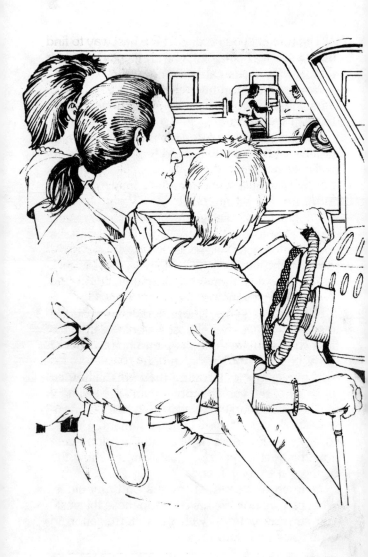

The three of you agree that the best way to find out if these men are the thieves is to wait until later that night and search the truck.

You let enough time pass for everyone to fall asleep before you, Slickrock, and Edward walk back to the truck.

"The locks are broken," you say. "I'm going to go inside. You two look around in the back."

While searching through the truck, you feel a tap on your shoulder. You jump, only to find it is Slickrock. He whispers to you, "We've found a whole bunch of pottery in the trailer. Let's go back to the motel. I don't want to get caught."

Back in the motel, the three of you decide to follow the men back to their base. Maybe you'll catch the leader behind this pottery theft outfit. These men could be just the hired hands.

When the first rays of the sun break the sky, you are sitting in the car keeping an eye on the truck. The men come out of their room. They quickly start the truck and drive down the road. You, Edward, and Slickrock follow them for many miles until you feel as if you're lost. Finally the truck turns onto a very narrow dirt road, leaving behind a cloud of dust.

Turn to page 92.

6

You spend the afternoon packing equipment and supplies needed for your expedition into the Escalante Canyon. It could be dangerous if you get lost. Edward calls Phillip Moss, your guide last summer, and asks him to come along with the two of you on the trip. He agrees. A Hopi Indian, Phillip has spent most of his life exploring the desolate and beautiful canyonlands of the Southwest.

When everything is packed and ready to go, the three of you pile into Edward's Jeep and head for Boulder, Colorado, where you'll begin your trip into the Escalante Canyon. There are few cars on the road, and the three of you trade off the driving, taking shifts. Seven hours later you reach Boulder. The local forest ranger, Alfred Wyatt, briefs you on where to go in the canyons.

"Those thieves made a raid just yesterday," Alfred tells you. "They attacked one of my favorite ruins. There's nothing left but a pile of rock and mud brick. It looks like a bomb exploded there."

"Could you tell us the location of this site?" you ask. "We might be able to find some clues. You never know."

Alfred hands you a large map. "I made this to show where the thieves have hit. I used my own set of symbols; this key explains what they mean. Good luck, and be careful. These thieves mean business. Don't get too close to them."

Go on to the next page.

It takes about an hour to reach the location. You leave the Jeep behind a large boulder as you hike the first few miles, the desert stretching before you. You're very tired. You aren't used to carrying a heavy load on your back, but once you reach the rim of the canyon, you get a burst of energy and excitement. Before you stretches a puzzlelike maze of large and small canyons. The yellow-orange rock and sand dazzle you with their beauty.

Turn to page 107.

8

Early the next morning Edward wakes you up. He is excited and sounds upset.

"The thieves have sent a note to the police demanding that they call off the investigation. They've threatened to take hostages from one of the smaller reservations. Come, let's get down to the station and see what we can find."

You jump out of bed and get dressed quickly. Edward is waiting for you in the Jeep, and together you roar off to his father's headquarters, even though Mr. Chinaua is not there. You locate the reports. There are many of them, and it takes you most of the day to go through them.

"Most of the raids have been made in the Escalante River region of Utah. I wonder why?" you ask.

"It's remote, I guess. What do you think about driving up there and having a look around?" Edward says. He loves adventure, and so do you.

"Great idea," you say. "Let's wait for your father to get back so he'll know where we are."

Turn to page 12.

The drive back to Shiprock is pleasant. You are happy to be back in the Southwest with Edward and excited by your leads and a chance to break the case. Arriving back in town, you go to the police station. The officer on duty tells you that Mr. Chinaua has gone home. You are to meet him there. When you reach Edward's house, Mr. Chinaua comes running out.

"Hurry up. You're just in time. There were more raids in the Grand Canyon. I'm going to take a raft down the Colorado River to check the ruins. You can join me if you want."

You explain to Mr. Chinaua about your conversation with Mr. Fiddleburn and the information he gave you.

"We should check those stores out when we get back," he says enthusiastically. "But it's up to you. I'm leaving now. You can either come with me or follow your leads."

Edward leaves the decision up to you.

If you decide to join Mr. Chinaua on the raft, turn to page 16.

If you decide to follow your own leads with Edward and meet with the pottery dealers, turn to page 24.

"Hey, what's going on—" you start to demand, but the look on Slickrock's face silences you. His features suddenly seem to be made out of stone.

You drive the rest of the way back to your Jeep in silence. Slickrock drops you off and barely mutters a farewell. You and Edward stand helplessly by the side of the road as he pulls away.

You feel certain you were on the verge of solving a much bigger mystery than the theft of the Anasazi pottery. But now, for some reason, your major lead has just evaporated into thin air!

Discouraged, you and Edward drive back to Shiprock. You spend the rest of the summer trying to solve the puzzle of the Anasazi raids, but despite many attempts to contact him, you never hear from Slickrock again.

The End

12

Mr. Chinaua is back soon. He approves, but suggests that you and Edward wait a day or two. He might be able to go with you then.

You're not sure what you and Edward should do. If you wait for Mr. Chinaua, you might be able to do some research over the next couple of days. On the other hand, the sooner you get to the Escalante River region of Utah, the sooner you may uncover some clues that will help save the ruins.

If you decide to wait for Mr. Chinaua,
turn to page 100.

If you decide to leave as soon as possible,
turn to page 6.

When you are finished, you stand up and ask the boy if he is all right. He is so frightened he is unable to speak.

Many people stand around, looking at you with amazement. There is silence among the Indians until one man finally steps forward.

"I do not know who you are, why you are here, or how you have found us, but I owe you my deepest gratitude," he says, offering you his hand. "You have saved my son's life today."

"I was only doing what I could. I accept your gratitude, but first I must apologize for following you in such a manner," you say.

Slickrock comes forward and speaks to the man in some kind of Indian dialect. They move aside together.

Turn to page 102.

14

The voice and the hand turn out to belong to a small Indian boy who hands you and Edward large candles.

Walking through the cave, you can hear voices at the other end. Suddenly you notice a bright light. The two of you walk out of the cave and into a beautiful valley.

"Welcome to the Anasazi Kingdom. Our home is called The Valley of Endless Light."

"This is the most beautiful place that I have ever seen," you respond automatically.

A few minutes later, Slickrock joins you at the entrance to the valley. He explains that this is the home of the Anasazi, where they have lived for the last five hundred years. As he explained to you on the river, the Aztecs came to capture the Anasazi long ago. Some managed to escape to this valley, although most were taken by the Aztecs.

"Why hasn't a plane ever spotted this valley before?" you ask.

"We are not sure what causes it, but there is a reflection of light that comes from the glaciers in the distant mountains. From the air it looks as though this valley is a barren, rocky plain."

Turn to page 110.

16

Mr. Chinaua waits in his pickup truck while you and Edward prepare to join him on the trip down the Colorado River. Finally, when all your gear is gathered, the three of you head for Moab, Utah, where you will hook up with your guide, Henry Beegay.

"Call me Slickrock," he says when you meet him. He is a strong, kind-looking Indian, and you take an immediate liking to him.

Early the next morning, Slickrock takes the three of you to his rafts by the river. It takes several hours to prepare them for your trip. The rafts are large and made of rubber. You steer them with two large paddles. Slickrock reviews the safety precautions necessary for traveling on the river.

By noon you push out into the large brown Colorado River. The current immediately grabs the rafts, taking control of them, leading you toward the Grand Canyon.

"On our first day the river will be easy. Tomorrow we will be reaching some large rapids," Slickrock calls, leading the way. On either side of you the walls of the Grand Canyon rise sharply. You can only see the blue sky when you look straight above you.

Go on to the next page.

"This is amazing. I never imagined that the canyon would be so deep," you tell Edward.

"Wait until two or three days from now. The canyon gets much deeper, and the river gets quite rough. We're in for a great ride," Edward says with a gleam in his eyes. He's been through the Grand Canyon before, so he knows what's in store for you.

Turn to page 105.

You climb into the helicopter and take off. From the large opening on one side, you and Edward scan the area below with the binoculars.

"To the right," you yell over the noise of the rotors. "Can you see him? He's just about to cross the river."

Mr. Chinaua responds quickly, but the man crosses the river and escapes into a small canyon.

"We'll have to wait until he comes out," Edward says.

Mr. Chinaua answers, "I'm going to try and get as close as possible. We've got loudspeakers and tear gas."

The helicopter gets close to the canyon. A figure jumps out from behind a rock, holding a rifle.

The first bullet flies through the cabin without hitting anybody. But a second bullet hits the blades above you. The helicopter spins and loses altitude in a sickening lurch. Within seconds it hits the floor of the canyon and explodes upon impact. It doesn't take long for the flames to incinerate all of you.

The End

20

Once you are back on the river, Slickrock says, "We have about two miles to go before we come to River's Revenge, some very large rapids. We'll pass through some large rapids on the way, but they'll seem small compared to this one."

"I've never run River's Revenge before," Edward says. "Last time we had to carry the raft and our gear around it. I'd really like to run it this time. I'm ready."

"Wait until we get to it," Mr. Chinaua says. "The river is very high, and the rapids might be larger than you remember. An injury on the river could be serious."

When you reach the rapids it looks very rough. You examine it with Edward and Slickrock. Slickrock tells you that he will run it if you want to, but Mr. Chinaua is going to walk around. The sound of the roaring water is both exciting and frightening. You're not sure if you want to take the risk, even if it might be fun.

If you decide to walk around the rapids,
turn to page 32.

If you choose to run the rapids,
turn to page 41.

Although you and Edward choose not to spend a year with the Indians, you are allowed to remain with them for several days. During this time they tell you that they hold this ceremony once a year. Until now nobody has ever discovered them. Slickrock serves as your guide with the Indians in much the same way that he served as your guide on the river. It is then that you realize that Slickrock is one of them—he is a descendant of the Anasazi!

"Why didn't you tell us this before?" you ask.

"We have remained hidden because we regard the modern world as a step backward from our civilization," Slickrock responds. "We wish to be left alone to live our lives our own way. When we first met you were not ready. I needed to know if you could be trusted."

Turn to page 28.

Tails it is, so you and Edward stay. Elk Mountain Mining can wait for now. According to Mr. Wyatt's map, you will come across three sites if you hike up into a nearby canyon called Coyote Gulch. Of the three sites, two have already been raided. The other, harder to find, is apparently untouched.

Coyote Gulch is one of the most beautiful side canyons that you have ever been in. A small stream meanders down the middle with large sandstone walls rising hundreds of feet above you.

"There's a large natural bridge across the canyon up ahead," Phillip says.

Reaching the bridge, you are amazed. It is about two hundred feet above your heads, wide enough for a person to walk across it. On a grassy bank below the arch, you see a small tent. A woman stands next to it.

"Phillip, is that really you?" she yells.

"Mary, what in the world are you doing here?" Phillip introduces you and Edward to Mary Simmons. She is the foremost anthropologist specializing in the Anasazi Indians. You have read many of her books and have always wanted to meet her.

Turn to page 67.

You regret giving up a trip on the Colorado River, but you want to follow up on your own leads.

Mr. Chinaua climbs into his pickup truck and heads off toward the river. You and Edward proceed to get in touch with the pottery dealers that Mr. Fiddleburn told you about.

"I've got a man on the phone who says he can meet with us at nine o'clock tomorrow morning," Edward announces eagerly.

"That's great. Tell him that we'll be there," you reply.

The pottery dealer is in Prescott, Arizona. Once again you will be spending quite a bit of time in the Jeep. You remind yourself to take some tapes along with you.

Turn to page 46.

You think quickly. "We've been in the canyons for over a week now. You're the first person that we've spoken to," you tell the old man.

"I've been in the canyons for much longer than that, and you are the first people that have bothered me. What do you want?" His voice is gruff, but not mean.

"We noticed your smoke signals. Were you sending a message?" Edward asks. "We saw another man doing the same thing. He is over on the other side of the canyon."

"I'm just rushing this fire to cook this rabbit," the man responds. Looking at it, you can tell that it was not shot. It looks as though it was killed with an atlatl, a cross between a bow and a catapult. You've seen samples in the museum in Santa Fe, but you know the weapon has not been used since the Anasazi disappeared.

"Did you use an atlatl?" you ask.

"Yes, I did. What's it to you?"

"We've been chasing a man whom we think is responsible for destroying Anasazi ruins, just like the one that you are standing next to." Edward pauses for a minute and then continues, "We thought that you and this man were signaling each other."

Turn to page 42.

"Edward," you whisper, "your dad's coming. Helicopter." You point upward.

"Let's just hope that guy stays put in the mine," he replies.

"Don't worry, even if he does leave, we'll be able to track him down with the helicopter," you say.

In less than an hour you hear the chattering of helicopter blades cutting through the air. The craft circles once, then settles down, raising a cloud of dust. The man runs out of the mine and sprints toward a nearby side canyon.

"He's escaping!" you yell. "Let's get him!"

Mr. Chinaua suggests that it would be best for you to go after the man on foot. That way, you could follow him even if he hid in narrow canyons where the helicopter could never land. On the other hand, the helicopter might intimidate the man into surrendering.

If you decide to chase the man with the helicopter, turn to page 19.

If you agree it would be better to go after the man on foot, turn to page 65.

Looking back, you try to remember all that Slickrock has told you about the Anasazi. While you are with him and the others, over the next three days, you and Edward are shown how they make their pottery and told the ways of their lives and those of their ancestors. When the three days are up, Slickrock gives each of you a beautiful pot recently made in the Anasazi fashion.

"You need not search for the Anasazi," he says. "They will always be around wherever you are. Take these pots and remember the times that we have spent together."

The End

You locate several pots inside the ruin that you are searching.

"I think we should hide the other pottery here and take only one each," Edward suggests.

"Good idea. Let's mark the ones that we take so we can return them after the men are arrested," you say.

The day seems to last longer than you expected. By the time you are ready to leave, the crew has gathered more than thirty pots.

"What do you do with the pottery after Mr. Belton has seen them?" you ask.

"We take them to New York City. There's an auction set up there. Big bucks," Frankie says, laughing. "Really big bucks."

"I'm familiar with New York," you say. "Maybe I could help. I know my way around there."

Frankie and Walt discuss this for a couple of minutes. "Okay, kid. We'll give you a try. In fact, I think you'll make an excellent cover." Pausing for a minute, he adds, "You might want to stay out here longer, though, and earn some more money. We're sending out another group Thursday."

You could stay for another dig and gather more evidence against Mr. Belton and Mr. Yardley. However, if you and Edward went to New York, maybe you could trap the whole ring of thieves.

If you go to New York City, turn to page 82.

If you go out with the thieves again, turn to page 36.

Railroad ties lead into the mine. You follow these for almost an hour. By this time you are deep under the earth's surface, and the only light you have is from your lamps. On your right-hand side you can see an opening. It is damp and cold in the shaft. Your imagination conjures up images of snakes, bats, and possibly even thieves.

"Let's go and look in there. I don't think that we're going to find anything by following these rails." Edward walks into the opening as you follow him.

"Look at this. I think somebody's living here," he says.

Your lamps scan the room. There is a bed and a pile of clothes.

"This certainly hasn't been sitting here since the mine was shut down over ten years ago." As you speak, you see something with the beam of your lamp. "Anasazi pottery!" you yell. "There must be over two dozen pots!"

"Let's hide the Jeep and stake this place out," Edward suggests.

Turn to page 49.

You decide not to run the rapids. It was a tough choice, but you are glad that you made it. Looking at the rapids while carrying your gear, you realize you might not have survived the run.

"I've never seen these rapids look so rough in all my years of running the river," Slickrock exclaims as you come out of River's Revenge.

Finally, the four of you are once again floating down the river. You are tired from carrying the raft and your gear, and your thoughts turn back to the destruction and theft of the Indian villages.

Two miles downriver from the rapids, Slickrock pulls ashore and turns off on a barely visible trail into the canyons. As you look at your map of the Anasazi sites in this area, you can't locate the one Slickrock is heading for.

"Trust me," he says. "I'm the only person who knows about these ruins. They're very special. I've never told anyone about them. Promise me to keep this to yourselves."

"Of course," you say, speaking for Edward and Mr. Chinaua.

When you finally arrive at the ruins, you are amazed. They are by far the most beautiful of the Anasazi sites you have ever seen. They are so well preserved, it looks as though they were built recently, not hundreds of years ago.

Turn to page 78.

"I think that the Anasazi were attacked by the Aztec Indians," Slickrock proposes. "The Aztecs were a very large tribe that lived in Mexico. They used human beings for their sacrifices to their gods. It's my belief that they captured the Anasazi and used them as sacrifices. I know this theory is unusual, but I feel it in my bones. These old villages talk to me of fear and death, as well as of the joy of their lives."

"Slickrock," you ask, "would you come with us to help in our search?"

Rubbing his chin with his thumb, Slickrock thinks for a moment, then answers, "I would love to join you. It would be my destiny."

"Then consider us a team," you say. "We are honored to have you join us."

"No, my friends," Slickrock answers thoughtfully. "It is all of us who honor the Anasazi."

Mr. Chinaua has to get back to Shiprock to finish a case, but you and Edward make plans with Slickrock to meet in Moab after your rafting trip has ended.

Turn to page 53.

Heads it is. You call Mr. Chinaua when you arrive back in town and ask him to have one of the police researchers collect information about the Elk Mountain Mining Company. He agrees, pleased with your work. It's a good start on a tough problem.

Arriving in Shiprock hours later, you say goodbye to Phillip Moss, go straight to tribal police headquarters and meet with Edward's dad.

"You don't know how glad I am . . ." Mr. Chinaua says, stopping in midsentence to pick up the phone. A moment later he announces, "There's been a shooting in one of the smaller villages, and I've got to go there. Sorry. You two go over that information on the mine, okay?" Grabbing his vest and badge, Mr. Chinaua rushes out to his cruiser, a 4 x 4 pickup.

Waiting for you in one of the conference rooms is a large pile of folders filled with newspaper clippings and odd bits of paper.

"It looks like we have our work cut out for us now," Edward says when he sees the pile. "You take half and I'll take half. Then we'll compare notes."

"Right," you agree with a shrug.

This is not the dramatic time that you had pictured, but you know that research is really important. All afternoon you read through the material without really finding out anything useful. At the end of the day you and Edward head home.

Turn to page 58.

Frankie leaves for the auction in New York, but Walt and Steve stay behind with you and Edward. You spend the next three days hunting the ruins for pottery. You and Edward get to know Walt fairly well, and he confides in you that he is only doing this because his wife is ill and he can't afford the medical bills. He seems genuinely ashamed of himself, so you decide to take a calculated risk and let Walt know who you are. He agrees to help you put Mr. Belton behind bars.

"We'll set up a meeting with Belton and have the tribal police tape it," you suggest.

"Belton is very suspicious. He can smell a cop a mile away," Walt says, shaking his head.

"It's too dangerous to do it on our own," you tell him insistently.

After arranging a meeting with Mr. Belton, you call the tribal police. They don't like the idea of you and Edward getting involved, but finally they agree, even though they think it is too risky.

The meeting goes very well. You get Mr. Belton to admit that he knows the digging up and sale of the pottery is illegal. He laughs and says, "Hey, life's illegal, what can I tell you. Politicians are dishonest, bankers are crooks, brokers are highway robbers. Me? I'm just a little guy who likes pottery. It's no big deal."

Go on to the next page.

Two days later the police arrest Mr. Belton. He isn't laughing when he is sentenced for his crimes.

The thing that really bothers you now is that the raids have still not stopped. "There must be somebody else out there stealing pottery," you tell Edward. "I think that we should go to the Escalante River region of Utah and begin again."

Turn to page 6.

"We'll have to tell Charlie Wanayo. He's in charge of the tribal police while my father is off on a case," Edward says as you pull into police head-quarters.

"Hey, Claudia. Can we see Charlie? Is he free?" Edward asks the secretary.

"Sure, he's in his office. Let me buzz him," Claudia responds.

A few minutes later you are in Charlie Wanayo's large, oak-paneled office. Edward describes the recent events and asks Charlie what to do about the pottery that you need to bring to tomorrow's meeting with Mr. Yardley.

Charlie is impressed with the work you have done and is eager to help you. "We've got pottery confiscated from a thief many years ago. It's down in the evidence room. Let me call down and tell them you're coming to borrow some."

"Thanks, Charlie. Thanks a lot," you say.

"Watch yourselves, you hear. Don't push him too far," Charlie adds. "Some of these dealers can be real nasty. Especially if your hunch is right."

You are led into a large room in the basement. There you are shown a whole shelf of pottery. Some are beautiful, perfectly formed pieces; others are broken and rough. "We need the best ones in order to make a good impression at our meeting."

One piece attracts your attention. It's a greenish pot with blue patterns of animals across the top. It's in such good condition it looks as though it was made only a few years ago.

Turn to page 87.

Four men hold rifles pointed at you, Edward, Phillip, and Mary. They bind and gag the four of you, put you in a van, and drive to a nearby town. Before long they stop at the Red Cactus Motel. The leader goes to the office and returns a few minutes later.

"We've paid for this room for the next six days and have asked the maid not to come and clean it. You won't be disturbed. Sorry, but it can't be helped. Pleasant dreams."

The four of you are dumped in the room and tied up. The smugglers, with a last laugh, leave. You hear their car drive off, knowing you will never see them again.

The End

Deciding to run the rapids, you try to figure out the safest route. A large whirlpool on the left-hand side of the river rules out that way. The center is full of rocks. It seems it will have to be the right-hand side.

Heart pounding, all senses alert, you start out for the rapids with Edward and Slickrock.

"Here we go," Slickrock yells.

You barely move forward when a huge wave splashes over your head, ripping the paddle from your hands. There is nothing that you can do now. The river has you in its control, the current pulling you toward the whirlpool. Round and round you spin until suddenly the raft is flipped over and you are pushed under. Looking up, you can see only water. It takes just a few seconds before you are pushed deeper and deeper into the whirlpool, but it is hours before your body washes ashore.

The End

"I don't have any idea what you're talking about," the old man says. "You can rest assured, youngsters, that I would never associate with people who destroy Anasazi ruins. And if I ever find them messing with my ruins, I'll kill them."

The smoke signals from the other side of the canyon have stopped, and the man you were chasing is no longer in sight.

You're not sure whether to believe the old man or not. Perhaps you should go back and look for the other man you were chasing. On the other hand, the old man might be involved in the raids. It might be better to stay with him and see what you can find out.

If you decide to look for the man you were following, turn to page 69.

If you decide to stay with the old man, turn to page 96.

The parachute and the crate can wait until later. Instead, Mary leads the three of you through deep underbrush for about a hundred yards. The going is rough, but finally you come upon a clearing. Against the walls of the cliff stands a group of beautiful Anasazi houses. They are only five or six feet high. The Anasazi were much smaller than the average person is today.

"Here we are," Mary tells you. "The pots are all in the buildings. Be careful where you step. Valuable pottery is everywhere around this site."

The largest house, you find, contains fifteen or twenty pots. They are in excellent condition, worth thousands of dollars to the thieves.

Coming out of the hut you see a strange footprint that does not belong to any of you.

"Look at this," you say to Phillip. "There's a trail of prints here. Let's follow them."

The footprints lead you to the mouth of a small cave.

"Shall we go in?" Mary asks.

"Why not?" you reply, trying to sound confident.

"I'm game. How about you, Phillip?" Edward asks.

"Count me in," he replies. Edward gathers all of your equipment, and the four of you enter the cave cautiously. The entrance is narrow, but it soon opens up into a large gallery.

Turn to page 75.

You and Edward sit back in shock. "That seems fair," you say, amazed at how cool you're able to remain. You're dealing with a criminal, you can feel it in your bones.

Mr. Belton pulls out his wallet and peels off a hundred one-hundred-dollar bills. They lie in a stack in front of you.

"There you go. Count 'em. They're real," he says, smiling. "Do you have any others? I like these pots."

"No, but we can get more. We know our way around the canyons," Edward replies.

You're shocked at Edward. You wonder if he realizes that you're getting in deeper by the minute.

"I'll tell you what. A couple of my boys are going out to get some pottery tomorrow. If you want, you can go with them and show them around the canyons. I'll give you two thousand dollars for every pot that you find." Mr. Belton seems pleased with himself.

This could be more dangerous than you bargained for.

Go on to the next page.

"Great, Mr. Belton," Edward replies. "We'll do it. Shall we meet your men here?"

"Yes. Tomorrow morning, early." He shakes hands and leaves.

Moments later, you telephone Edward's father from a pay phone on the corner. He's not there, but Henry, the deputy, takes down the information and offers to join you in the morning. "It could get dangerous," Henry says. "But it's up to you."

If you decide to go alone with the men tomorrow, turn to page 54.

If you ask the deputy to join you, turn to page 59.

Waking at five with the early sun, you can feel that it is going to be a very hot day. "The man we will be meeting with is Thomas Yardley," Edward tells you. "He is the owner of Forgotten Treasures, an antique shop specializing in Indian artifacts."

"Maybe it should be called Forbidden Treasures," you say, laughing.

It's only eight in the morning when you arrive in Prescott. Over breakfast you plan what you will say to Mr. Yardley.

"I think we should pretend that we have pottery to sell, like we did with Mr. Fiddleburn. It worked once, why not again?" Edward says.

You agree, and the two of you walk over to Mr. Yardley's shop and wait outside for him to arrive.

Turn to page 52.

Slickrock's cousin lives less than three miles away. He'll be back as soon as he can. Watching the men load the trailer, you and Edward glance nervously at your watches, hoping that Slickrock returns in time. Within the hour the men finish, climb into their truck, and drive off, a cloud of dust following them, marking their trail.

"This is it," Edward says. "We've lost them now." But before he can finish speaking, you see a car racing down the road at high speed. It's Slickrock. "Hurry up," he yells, opening the door.

You climb in. "Which way?" Slickrock asks.

"Due south. See the dust cloud? That's them," you reply.

After twenty miles you spot the truck pulled over on the side of the road, steam rising from the radiator.

"Let's stop and ask if they need help," Edward suggests. "We'll act real neighborly!"

"No, let's pass them and wait for someone else to help them. We can't let them see us now," Slickrock counters.

You're not sure what to do, but the decision is left up to you.

If you choose to pull over and offer to help, turn to page 56.

If you decide to wait for the men down the road, turn to page 88.

Sitting on the roof of one of the buildings near the mine, you and Edward take turns watching the entrance. It is night now, and you are glad you brought along the infrared binoculars that enable you to see in the dark. You sleep while Edward takes his shift.

"Wake up. I think our thief has come home," Edward whispers in your ear as he shakes you. "I see someone climbing over the hill next to the conveyor belt."

"Hand me the binoculars," you say.

Looking through the binoculars, you see a man. He is carrying a very large sack. Maybe it's filled with pottery, you think. It's hard to make out any details too clearly.

"You keep watch," you tell Edward. "I'll call your dad. Maybe he'll send some help. We can't arrest this guy, we don't have the authority."

"Hurry," Edward replies.

Unfortunately, the closest phone is over seventy-five miles away. It's a long, bumpy trip in the Jeep.

"I'll use the new helicopter," Mr. Chinaua says over the phone. He sounds excited and eager.

Returning to the mine, you can't find Edward at first. Then you see him—he's climbed into one of the little railroad car buckets formerly used to bring ore out of the mine. Slowly you move toward him, careful not to make any noise. Finally you reach him.

Turn to page 26.

Edward attaches the rope to the harness around his waist and begins to climb the rock. He places pitons and chocks at intervals and hooks into them with the carabiner, an oval-shaped snap link. You feed the rope out to him little by little. Even if he does slip, you can at least help break his fall.

When Edward gets to the top you begin the climb. Finally you join him and gaze down at the floor of the canyon, five hundred feet below. You're glad that you didn't look down earlier.

Turn to page 84.

"Sorry I'm late," Mr. Yardley says, opening the door of his store. "I had to take care of some important business." After introductions are made, the three of you sit down in a large office jammed with pottery, rugs, kachina dolls, dance masks, and trays of silver jewelry.

"What can I do for you? Are you buying or selling?" he asks.

"We've been camping in the canyons, and we found some Anasazi pottery. We were wondering if it would be possible to sell them."

"Well, well, well. . . . I don't get offers like this very often, but I just might be able to help you." Mr. Yardley fiddles with a letter opener as he contemplates your offer. "Bring the pottery to me. I'll show them to a friend of mine who might be interested in buying them. Why don't you come back tomorrow. You can meet my friend then."

Mr. Yardley leads you out of his store. "I'll see you tomorrow. Bring anything you've got." Mr. Yardley smiles. He is almost smirking.

"I think that we may have hit the jackpot," you say to Edward on your way home. "All we have to do now is get our hands on some Anasazi pottery." The two of you are excited. You never imagined that things would fall into place so quickly.

Turn to page 38.

You and Edward drive toward Moab from Shiprock after you drop Mr. Chinaua off. "I really think we're going to do it," you say. "I think the three of us are going to catch the thieves and solve the mystery of the Anasazi."

Slickrock is equally excited. When you pick him up in Moab, he is ready to go.

"Lead the way," you offer, and for the next hour you travel along the dusty edges of the desert.

"Where are we headed?" Edward asks Slickrock.

"We are going into the heart of the canyonlands," he answers.

Before long you reach a point where you can no longer use the Jeep.

"Okay, this is where we carry our packs," Slickrock says as he lifts his backpack and slips his arms through the straps.

As the three of you enter the canyons, the trail disappears. You use your compass and topographical maps, and Slickrock uses his instincts. The land around you is dry and rocky. The sun is hot, and the air scratches your lungs. When the sun begins to set, you make camp and cook dinner over a small gas stove. Everything around you is quiet and beautiful. Stars begin to appear slowly, and then all at once they seem to fill the night sky. Before long you sleep well, knowing you are on your way.

Turn to page 68.

You thank Henry but tell him you prefer to continue the job on your own.

You find it hard to sleep. The idea that you and Edward are about to go out alone into the desert with a group of crooks sends chills down your spine. You are both fearful and excited.

At dawn you arrive at Forgotten Treasures. The white van Mr. Belton told you to watch for is there when you arrive, along with three men, Frankie, Walt, and their Indian guide, Steve. They don't appear to be dangerous, but you keep on your guard.

"We'll be traveling deep into the backlands of New Mexico. Steve here tells us that there are a lot of Anasazi sites in that area," Walt says. "Belton says you know a lot about this stuff, right?"

"I've been down there before, and I can show you some really good sites," Edward responds. This pleases the men, but you sense that they don't exactly like having the two of you with them. The guide, Steve, seems particularly displeased.

The drive is long and bumpy; the day uncomfortably hot. Once on the trail, you ask the men how much pottery they have found for Mr. Belton.

"We've only been doing this work for a couple of months, but we have already found about a hundred pots so far. We've hit maybe six, seven sites," Frankie answers.

Go on to the next page.

This information fits in perfectly with recent occurrences, both the time period and the number of Anasazi sites that have been raided.

Steve leads you to an Anasazi ruin hidden in a small canyon. The sun's rays don't penetrate the deep niche in the earth at this time of day, and the canyon is dark and cool. You and Edward search one area while everyone else digs up the floor of two small dwellings. The sound of the shovels and pickaxes upsets you, knowing the damage they are causing.

Turn to page 29.

As Slickrock pulls the car over onto the soft, sandy shoulder of the road, you roll down your window and call one of the men over. "Howdy. Do you folks need any help? Can we give you a ride into town?"

It is the first time you have come face-to-face with the thieves. The man looks at all of you, his eyes widening when he sees Slickrock.

Suddenly you feel that something strange is going on. Sure enough, the man says something to Slickrock in a language you don't understand. You are almost positive it is some Indian dialect, but one you are not at all familiar with.

Abruptly Slickrock gets out of the car. You and Edward remain inside as he and the man take a walk a short distance away, conversing intently. Then Slickrock returns, gets in, slams the door, and drives quickly off.

Turn to page 11.

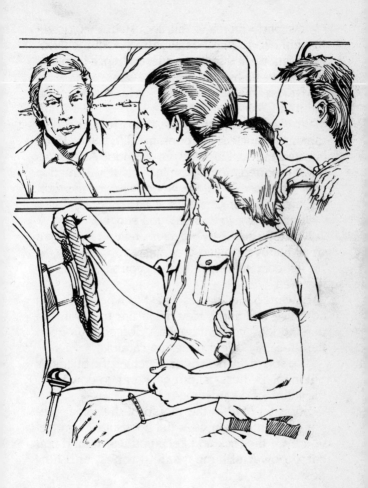

"Did you read that article about why they closed the mine?" Edward asks you over dinner. Edward's mom died six years ago, and since then he's learned to be a good cook.

"I guess I missed that article. Why *did* they close the mine?" you respond.

"It was a uranium mine that produced plutonium for nuclear weapons. In 1978 it was closed because the quality of the ore was poor. At least, so it was reported. Some people think they wanted to wait until prices went up. Nobody has been working the mine for years. It's still abandoned."

"Let's take a look at it," you suggest.

It's a long haul, but two days later you stand on a small hill overlooking the mine.

"It's really spooky out here," you say, surveying the area.

Edward parks the Jeep next to what looks like an office building. "Hey, fresh tire tracks in the parking lot," you announce. "Somebody's been here recently. We'd better be careful."

You spend the next hour searching the buildings but in vain. "Let's get our gear and go down into the mine," Edward suggests.

Soon you are at the mouth of the mine, prepared to enter. You wear full bodysuits to protect you from the rock and keep you warm, and you carry powerful lamps, safety ropes, and harnesses.

Turn to page 31.

"Okay," you tell Henry. "Come along."

The following morning, the deputy joins you and Edward. Arriving at Forgotten Treasures, you see Mr. Belton's men sitting in a white van as you pull up next to it. As Henry approaches the van, one of the men yells out, "It's a setup. That man's a cop! Beat it!"

The van pulls out, spraying dirt and gravel in an arc that rattles against your Jeep.

"I blew our cover," Henry says, slamming his fist on the dashboard. "I'm sorry. I shouldn't have come."

You're unable to tail the van, which quickly disappears down the road. You know where to find Mr. Yardley and Mr. Belton, but from now on the case is in the hands of Mr. Chinaua and the tribal police.

The End

Backtracking through the narrow passage, you find a small opening, just large enough to squeeze through. After worming your way through, you eventually end up in a tiny cavern. A muffled sound comes from one of the corners. You notice an Indian woman cowering in the darkness.

"Please don't hurt me," she sobs. "I didn't mean to run away, but you frightened me."

"We won't hurt you. We're hiding ourselves," you respond, attempting to calm the woman down.

She seems to think you are some men she has run away from, perhaps those whose voices you heard. "I am confused. Please tell me who you are."

You explain, but she still does not seem to believe you. You shine the light on your faces so she can see that you are not the ones she is hiding from.

Finally the woman calms down. Relaxing, she begins to tell you her story. Her name is Josephine Beegay, and she comes from the Four Winds Tribe of the Navaho Indians. The pottery thieves had taken her and her family hostage in an attempt to force them to reveal other Anasazi ruins. Last night she escaped when they were camping in Coyote Gulch. "I was very scared," she tells you. "They came searching through the canyons, and they tracked me here. They are horrible people. Murderers. Many years ago, my grandfather brought me here and showed me this cave. My people used it for safety. Now I must do the same."

Turn to page 97.

Returning to the rafts, you, Edward, and Mr. Chinaua explain to Slickrock that you are trying to catch the thieves and stop them from destroying the sites. You also explain to him that you hope to find out what really happened to the Anasazi Indians, and why they mysteriously disappeared.

Slickrock listens to what you have to say and then carefully replies, "I have tried to figure out the same thing myself. I have spent quite a lot of time studying the Anasazi and their way of life. After all my research, I think I have come up with a valid theory as to why they disappeared so suddenly."

"Can you share it with us?" you ask.

Turn to page 33.

"Swim for your life," Edward yells to you as the flood hits, carrying the two of you down the canyon. Before you know it you are caught up in the turbulent water, and there is no chance for escape.

You lose sight of Edward, and then you are brutally thrown against a large, sharp rock. The world dims as a gauzy haze covers your eyes. . . .

The End

Slowly the four of you creep back out the passage, trying to make as little sound as possible. The voices are getting closer. You have a feeling that whoever is there, isn't in the cave for enjoyment. Reaching the main gallery, you move slowly toward the mouth of the cave, hiding behind some stalactites.

"Look at that, Joe," a rough voice comes from behind you. "Don't they look a little large to be pack rats living in a cave?" You turn around and see six lamps shining in your eyes. "They must have followed us," one of them says.

"I think that we should get rid of them," another suggests. "I have an idea."

With that you are taken deeper into the cave, where you, Edward, Phillip, and Mary are left without your lamps. You don't know who these men are or what they are doing in the cave, but in the total darkness, you know you will never be able to find the answer—or your way out.

The End

It will be tough to catch up with the man. He has a good head start, but you decide to go after him on foot. Mr. Chinaua waits with the helicopter as you and Edward grab your packs from the Jeep. At the rim of the canyon you spot the man. He's headed toward the Grand Canyon, only about a half mile away. You'll never find him if he reaches it, you think.

"We have to hurry. If he gets to the Grand Canyon, there are literally thousands of places he can hide," you say, gasping for breath between each word.

"Look, he's running up that sandy bank toward the mesa on the other side of the canyon. We might be able to save time if we climb up this rockface and head him off. It's steep, but it's quick," you say.

"Good idea, but do we have enough gear?" Edward responds.

"Yeah, I have everything in my pack. Let's go."

Reaching the base of the rock wall, you unpack your climbing equipment—ropes, harnesses, safety helmets, pitons, and chocks. You don't have time to switch to the special climbing shoes with rubber soles.

Looking up, you see large black clouds dotting the sky. If it rains while you are on the rockface, the two of you will be in grave danger. A good grip on the rock is almost impossible when it's wet and slippery.

Turn to page 51.

That evening, after you have set up camp next to Mary's, you talk about the thievery and destruction of the Anasazi ruins. Mary asks if she can join you. Without a moment's hesitation, the three of you eagerly accept her offer and tell her where you are planning to go. She will be a very valuable asset to your team.

Early the following morning, Mary leads the three of you to the third site. She says it's one of the best examples of Anasazi architecture in this region. At the site are pots that represent all the different stages of Anasazi pottery, a period that spans hundreds of years.

Suddenly the drone of an airplane engine overhead breaks the silence of the canyon. Looking up, you see a large plane. It's an old DC–3, a model that was built before World War II and still flies better than many modern planes. A crate falls from the plane, and a parachute quickly opens. It descends rapidly, landing on the mesa about a mile away. The crate will most likely be there when you get back. But instead of continuing to explore the Anasazi site, perhaps you should track the crate down and see what's inside.

If you decide to go examine the cargo, turn to page 85.

If you choose to continue on to the Anasazi site, turn to page 43.

The next thing you know, it is morning.

"Up and at 'em. We have only a short hike to the first Anasazi ruins. Let's not waste any time," Slickrock says, standing over you. He hands you and Edward a large thermos of hot chocolate each.

With a groan the two of you crawl out of your sleeping bags. After breakfast, you all set off into a large canyon, following a small stream that runs through it.

"According to the map that Mr. Chinaua gave me," Slickrock tells you and Edward, "the thieves haven't touched any of the sites in this canyon."

"Hey, look!" you say, pointing to three men leading heavily loaded horses in the distance. "We have company."

Slickrock seems unalarmed. "Tourists, I'll bet. Pilgrims, we call them," he says with a grin. You watch as the men and horses head away.

Turn to page 93.

You decide to turn around and look for the other man. The climb down into the canyon is very rough. There are loose stones everywhere, and it is steep.

Upon reaching the floor of the canyon, you and Edward set out across the wide sandy flat. Rain begins to fall, slowly at first. Then a thunderstorm erupts. A shallow river runs along the other side of the canyon. Suddenly you hear a rumbling sound louder and distinctly different than the thunder.

"It's a flash flood," you yell.

Although it rarely rains in the desert, when it does, water drops from the sky and fills the dry washes and arroyos. The rumbling gets louder. A large wall of brown water rushes toward you like a tidal wave. There is nowhere to escape.

Turn to page 62.

The plan is set; Mary will put on Josephine's clothes and meet with the thieves at the place where the river forks. But first Edward and Phillip will go for the tribal police. You will all meet up by the river.

"Are you sure you want to go through with this, Mary?" you ask as you sit and wait for the police to arrive.

"Yes, I want to do anything that I can to help put those thieves behind bars," Mary responds.

Three hours later Edward and Phillip arrive with the police. Disguised as Josephine, Mary sits on a small boulder by the river, waiting for the thieves. Three men walk up the canyon and, seeing her, yell, "It's about time you decided to cooperate. We were just about to work your family over."

Unfortunately, when the men get closer, one of them yells, "It's not her. We've been tricked." They scatter throughout the canyon, but it doesn't take long for the police to round them up. Josephine is very thankful to all of you for saving her and re-uniting her family. For now you can only hope that this puts an end to the senseless raids on these silent villages of long ago.

The End

After hours of searching, Hank, one of the deputies, finally finds the markers. The six of you jump onto your horses and follow the markers up the canyon.

"We must be getting close now," you say. "Slickrock and Edward are on foot, and we're making good time on these horses."

"Look there!" shouts Mr. Chinaua. "The trail leads out of the canyon. Let's hurry. I really want to put the cuffs on those thieves."

Riding as fast as possible, the six of you leave the canyon and gallop across the mesa. Slickrock and Edward are just visible in the distance, signaling you with raised arms.

Reaching them you ask, "Where are they?"

"They're gone! They drove off in a truck only an hour ago. The truck didn't have any license plates on it, and they'll probably ditch it soon. We're out of luck!" Edward says angrily. "We're back to square one."

It's not easy after all of your efforts, but you realize you have to press on. You have the rest of your summer vacation ahead of you and hundreds of years of history to protect.

The End

You remain with the Anasazi, continuing to learn their ways and their history. After a year you and Edward are able to leave and visit your families, but you eventually decide to return to the valley, where you live for the rest of your lives.

The End

"Look at those stalactites," you say. "Watch your head. They're hanging down everywhere."

Many passages lead from the main gallery, and you have trouble deciding which one to take. Finally, for lack of any real reason, Edward suggests one that leads off to the right. It is so small that you have to crawl on your stomachs. The ground is muddy, making a squishy sound with every move that you make. As you proceed forward, your headlamps create eerie shadows in the tomblike space.

"See anything, Edward? Any footprints?" you ask.

"No, I can't see anything. But let's explore a little farther before we turn back," he says.

"I can hear voices," Phillip says.

"Probably just an echo," you reply, but a shiver of fear runs up your back.

"No, listen. I'm sure it's not an echo," Phillip says.

"Those voices are getting closer. Let's get out of here," whispers Edward.

"No, let's stay and find out who these people are," Mary suggests.

If you decide to hide, turn to page 60.

If you think that you can leave the cave without being heard, turn to page 64.

"Leave a good trail, you guys," you say, deciding to go for help.

"Don't worry," Slickrock says as they leave to follow the men. Staring after them, you suddenly feel alone and vulnerable. You'll feel better after you make some headway. The hoofprints of the horses will also serve as a good trail to follow, you remind yourself. You have nothing to worry about.

The hike back seems to pass very quickly, but the nearest town is fifty miles away, and the roads are bad. When you finally reach the town you call Mr. Chinaua from a pay phone in front of a gas station.

"Mr. Chinaua, we found them! We found them!" you shout over the phone. "Send help."

"Stay where you are. We'll be there," he says, sounding excited.

Sitting in a small diner several hours later, you see Mr. Chinaua pull up in his truck. There is a large horse trailer attached to it.

"I have four men with me and enough horses for all of us. Lead the way," he says.

Turn to page 91.

With a sheepish grin, the man mumbles under his breath, "Yes, I am. I had hoped that nobody would ever find me."

Sitting around the fire, Everett tells you that he was hiking in the canyons many years ago and decided that he never wanted to leave. Civilization had just become too much for him. For the last fifty-odd years, he has explored the canyons, paying painstaking attention to the Anasazi ruins.

Once he starts talking, Everett doesn't stop, and you and Edward sit with him long into the night, fascinated by him and his knowledge of the Anasazi Indians. Forgotten are the thieves, the man you were chasing, and your daily lives. For the time being, you are wrapped up in the past this old hermit is able to evoke.

The End

"How did you find these?" you ask Slickrock.

"I read about them in the journal of John Wesley Powell," he answers. "Do you know who he is?"

"Wasn't he the first man to take a boat down the Colorado River, over a hundred years ago?"

Slickrock looks at you with surprise. "Yes, he was. And in his journal he wrote about these ruins. Nobody else has ever been able to find them."

The small mud houses blend in with the cliffs, perfectly camouflaged. Inside the ruins are beautiful pots. You pray that thieves never find them. They belong here in the canyon where the Anasazi left them. There is a timelessness to this spot, a majesty that makes you feel calm and at peace with the world.

You take a few photographs and brush away your footprints so that the site is left exactly as you found it.

Turn to page 61.

You decide it's safer to stick together. The others agree. "We can't afford to let them see us," you say. "But I have another plan. We keep on their tail as far as possible. Hopefully, they'll lead us all the way to their hideout. For now, we'll just take it one step at a time."

"Then let's get going. They are getting farther away from us every second we sit here," Edward says.

Following the men proves to be an easy task. They move slowly, and the three of you stay far enough behind them, managing to keep out of sight. That night you set up camp about two miles from where the thieves are resting, taking turns keeping watch. For two more days you repeat this process until the thieves finally reach a road.

"Oh, no!" you exclaim. "Look, they've got a truck with a horse trailer! What now?"

"Let me look at the map," Slickrock says. "I have a cousin who lives in this area. Maybe I can borrow a car."

"Let's not waste any time," you say. "It won't take them long to load their horses and gear into the trailer."

Turn to page 48.

Mary and Phillip stay hidden with Josephine inside the cave while you and Edward sneak out, undetected.

Waiting on a ledge above the cave, you watch for the men to come out.

"I wonder what they're doing," Edward says. As he speaks, four men emerge from the mouth of the cave. Each is carrying a large bundle.

"Come, let's follow them," you tell Edward.

The men hurry down Coyote Gulch to the Escalante River. Several canoes lie hidden under some brush.

"What now? We don't have a canoe," Edward says.

"Let's wait and see what they do. There's only four of them. Maybe they'll leave a canoe behind."

You and Edward wait in the bushes while the men prepare their canoes. You were right, they only load two canoes. "We're in luck," you whisper to Edward as they push off.

Ten minutes later you and Edward head into the river's current in the remaining canoe. The heavy rains of recent days have swelled the river. The current is swift, and rocks and sandbars threaten your fragile craft.

The Escalante River flows into Lake Powell, a large reservoir built back in the nineteen-sixties. You continue along, maneuvering as best you can.

"I see the men. They're paddling across the lake," Edward says.

Turn to page 109.

The next day you and Edward fly to New York with Frankie and Walt. Mr. Chinaua has returned from his investigation and arranged for the FBI to give you help if you need it in New York.

"We'll be having a big auction tomorrow at the Gorham Hotel," Frankie tells you as you ride in from JFK Airport in a limousine. "The auction's been advertised for two weeks. It'll be easy big bucks for all of us."

A quick call to the FBI is all you need to arrange for them to raid the auction and arrest the thieves. In the meantime you and Edward help Frankie and Walt forge the documents necessary for the auction.

The auction turns out to be a big success. Hundreds of people eagerly await the beginning of the sale. Suddenly ten government men stand up and announce that this is an auction of stolen goods. A murmur runs through the crowd as people push to get out.

The thieves are arrested on charges of forgery and dealing in stolen antiquities. When the case has been closed, you return the pottery to its rightful site in the desert. Unfortunately there are still burial grounds that pottery is being stolen from, but the summer is over, and you must get back to school.

The End

"How did he get over there?" you exclaim in astonishment when you see the man standing on the opposite side of the canyon.

"Don't let him see us. We can still catch him." You lie down on your stomachs and watch the man through the binoculars. Time passes—fifteen minutes, then an hour.

"I'm beginning to feel like we're on a bird-watching trip, not chasing some thief," you tell Edward. Then he grabs your arm.

"Look, smoke signals. The guy's making smoke signals. What is he, some kind of nut?" Edward says.

Sure enough, you can see the man holding a blanket over a small fire. The smoke rises into the night sky in small puffs.

"I can see another set of signals," you say. "Look, they're coming from our side of the canyon, about a mile away from us. Let's go investigate."

Turn to page 94.

You head toward the fallen crate. Once you are out of the canyon, you can see the parachute in the distance. When the wind blows, the parachute fills with air and looks like a hot-air balloon. It takes only a few more minutes of walking before the four of you reach the crate.

"Let's pry the top off and see what's inside," you suggest.

The wooden top is hard to get off, but finally it yields. Inside is a thick layer of plastic foam. Underneath are hundreds of Anasazi pots wrapped in plastic.

"There must be millions of dollars' worth of pottery here," Edward says, awed. "The people flying the plane must have needed to ditch it for the moment."

"How correct you are," comes a voice in a thick accent from behind you. "Now, put your hands above your heads and turn around."

Turn to page 39.

You choose several other beautiful pots and carefully pack them into padded boxes. "Let's drive back to Prescott tonight and spend the night in a hotel," you suggest. "We can ask around town and see if we can find out anything about the Forgotten Treasures shop."

"Better to be prepared," Edward agrees.

You are lucky with your investigation. The people in Prescott talk freely about Forgotten Treasures. You find out that Mr. Yardley is just an employee of a rich businessman who owns the store. It is rumored that the real owner of the store has criminal connections.

Knowing this, you are wary when you enter the store. Mr. Yardley welcomes you and introduces you to his friend, Mr. Belton. "Here's the man I was telling you about. Did you bring the pottery?"

"Yardley tells me that the two of you may have some pottery that I might be interested in purchasing." Mr. Belton talks very slowly, with an accent you can't quite place. "Can I see them?"

You notice the diamond ring on his pinky. It's large, and from the way it reflects the morning sunlight, you know it's real. This man means business, you're sure of that. "Here they are," you say, opening the box and removing the pottery.

Mr. Belton's eyes open wide, sparkling like his diamond. "I'm impressed. These are good. Very good. I'll give you ten thousand dollars for all of them."

Turn to page 44.

You drive past the truck, keeping your eyes forward to avoid looking suspicious. About a half a mile later, Slickrock pulls over on a small dirt road and parks the car behind some bushes.

"Let's hike back and watch," Edward suggests.

Sitting on top of a small hill, you watch the men tinkering with their truck. About an hour later one of them gets behind the wheel and starts the engine.

"Hurry," Slickrock calls. The three of you double-time it back to the car.

You watch from behind the bushes as the truck passes, then follow from a distance. Almost a hundred miles later, the truck pulls into a motel. The men quickly enter the office, then return to the truck to get their bags.

"It looks like they're going to spend the night," Slickrock says. "There's another motel down the road. Let's go and get a room for ourselves. But first I think maybe we ought to try and find out if these men are the thieves. We really don't have any hard evidence yet."

Turn to page 5.

"My father is waiting for us in Shiprock," Edward says. "He'll explain everything then."

The drive between Albuquerque and Shiprock is beautiful—mountains to the east and north; desert and big sky all around. When you pull into the driveway, you see Mr. Chinaua sitting on the porch waiting for you. He has a large glass of lemonade in his hand.

"Welcome, my friend. I knew you would come. Here, have some lemonade to fight the heat. We have a lot to talk about."

You take a glass and sit down.

Several hours later, as you settle in for sleep, you think about everything that Mr. Chinaua has told you. The situation looks grim. It seems that there are several gangs raiding the Indian sites. And threats have been made to a volunteer citizens' patrol.

"Ed, let's go down to your father's office tomorrow and look at the reports," you say. "You never know. Maybe we'll find something that others have missed."

"I think that's about all that we can do at this point. I'll wake you up early tomorrow," Edward says. "Good night. And, hey, thanks for coming."

Turn to page 8.

You drive into the desert as far as you can with the horse trailer, then prepare the horses for the ride that lies ahead of you.

With the horses saddled up, the six of you head off into the canyons. It's getting dark now, but you push on. Time is of the essence, and you all know it. It doesn't take you long to find the trail of yellow ribbons. Slickrock was right when he said not to worry.

For the first couple of miles it is quite easy for you to follow the trail, but suddenly you reach a point where you lose sight of the markers.

"Everybody off your horses! Spread out! There has to be a marker nearby," Mr. Chinaua says. You are already off your horse and searching.

Turn to page 72.

The dirt road leads you deeper into the desert. You are now in southern Colorado, very close to the Anasazi ruins known as Cliff Palace, the largest group of dwellings that have been discovered. As you drive over the crest of a small hill, you see that the truck has stopped.

"We'll have to follow on foot from here," you say.

The better part of the day is spent following the men. You are very thankful for Slickrock's tracking abilities; you're able to keep up with them easily.

"Maybe they're leading us to an arranged sale of the pottery," Edward suggests. "If they are, we can arrest them on the spot."

"With what authority?" you ask. "We're not cops. This isn't a kids' game. These guys could be murderers."

"I'm a deputy in the tribal police," Slickrock says. "Don't worry. We'll play it safe. But let's wait until we see what they're doing before we make our move." He seems more cautious, you notice.

The sky begins to turn red as the men enter a large canyon. An amazing sight awaits you. There are hundreds of Indians all dressed in ceremonial robes. Slickrock suddenly relaxes and breaks into a grin, shaking his head at some private joke. The three of you sneak up as close as you can and hide behind a clump of sagebrush.

Turn to page 98.

By the time you get there, the first ruin on your map has been ransacked. Fresh tracks, hoofprints from horses, lead out to the desert. The men that you saw must have been the thieves!

You come up with two plans. The first is that all three of you will follow the thieves; the second is that Slickrock and Edward will follow the thieves while you go and get help. They will leave a trail of yellow ribbons tied to the trees so that you can follow them.

If you choose to go with Edward and Slickrock to follow the men, turn to page 80.

If you decide to go for help alone, turn to page 76.

What seems like only a mile between you and the column of smoke turns out to be a long hike. The going is rough. You have to climb up and down, over gullies and hills. The smoke signals continue as you travel, long into the night.

Eventually you reach a spot where you see the source of the signals. A man stands over a fire in front of a large cliff dwelling left by the Anasazi. Nestled underneath the overhanging cliff stand four beautiful Anasazi houses that appear to be in near-perfect condition. The man is big, with a bushy gray beard. You can tell he is not young.

You and Edward approach with caution since this man may have been warned against the two of you by the man you were chasing. He seems not to notice you.

"Hello," you say, quietly.

The man replies with a grunt.

Turn to page 25.

You decide to stay with the old man. Edward talks with him while you investigate the ruins. Inside one of the ancient buildings you find a beautiful old silver watch hanging on a stick that protrudes from a mud brick wall. On the back of this watch an inscription reads, *For my son, Everett Reuss, on his twenty-first birthday, 19—* The last two numbers are worn away. You sit back, shocked at your finding.

Everett Reuss, as you know from your research, disappeared in the Escalante Canyon over fifty years ago. Despite many attempts to find him, nobody was ever able to come up with even the smallest clue revealing his whereabouts. With a sudden burst of excitement, you run back to the fire.

"Are you Everett Reuss?"

Turn to page 77.

You offer Josephine your jacket. It is cold inside the cave and very damp.

"They have my family. I'm afraid they might hurt them." Josephine breaks into tears when she tells you this. "When I was in the small tunnel, they shouted that I have to meet them at the place where the river forks if I ever want to see my family alive again."

Mary interrupts to make a suggestion to the woman. "You and I look similar enough that we might be able to fool them. Perhaps I can use your clothes and meet with the thieves."

"Oh no, I could never allow you to endanger yourself on my behalf," Josephine says.

"Edward and Phillip will run as fast as they can and get the tribal police. I'll be fine. Don't worry," Mary replies.

"That could be dangerous, Mary," you say. "Maybe Edward and I should hide and then follow these people. Perhaps they'll lead us to Josephine's family."

At a loss for another idea, the others leave the decision up to you.

If you'd rather have Mary pretend to be Josephine, turn to page 70.

If you and Edward decide to follow the thieves, turn to page 81.

The men that you have been following enter the group of Indians. They put on the ceremonial robes and open up the bundles of pottery that they have been carrying. When this is completed, they gather in a large circle with the others and begin to perform a ritual dance.

"What's the dance?" you ask Slickrock.

"My grandfather first showed me it when I was very young," he says softly. "It is called the Dance of the Ancient Ones."

This surprises you because both the Hopi and the Navaho Indians refer to the Anasazi as the "Ancient Ones." Could this ceremony actually be one that the Anasazi performed many hundreds of years ago? you ask yourself.

The three of you edge quietly toward the circle of Indians. When you get closer you look at the robes that they are wearing. Because they are so worn, they are unlike usual ceremonial robes. They look almost like their everyday uniform, except for the ancient design.

Turn to page 112.

100

You decide to wait the two days for Mr. Chinaua. He is busy with other cases, so you and Edward go off to do some sleuthing on your own. "Let's check the stores that sell Indian pottery," you suggest. You know that if ancient Indian pottery is found on private land, the owner can legally sell it if he can provide documentation. Pottery from the public land—the Anasazi sites on reservations and national and state parkland—cannot be sold.

Santa Fe is your first target. Mr. Fiddleburn, the owner of The Golden Pot, which specializes in Anasazi pottery, reluctantly invites you into his office for a chat. You can see that he doesn't take the two of you seriously.

"What can I help you with today?" he asks.

"We want information about Anasazi pottery. We found a pot up in the canyonlands of Utah and wondered if you know anybody who would be willing to buy it."

Mr. Fiddleburn appears nervous.

"I don't deal in stolen pottery. You two had better leave, now. I don't like your kind."

"Wait a minute, please, Mr. Fiddleburn," you insist. "We are working for the tribal police. Could you please help us?"

Go on to the next page.

Mr. Fiddleburn calms down. Maybe he is honest, you think.

He looks through some papers and gives you the names of several shops that have been known in the past to sell stolen pottery. "Don't connect my name with this information. I could get in a lot of trouble. I don't know why I'm telling you this, but I can't stand what's going on. They're destroying what's left of the Anasazi. I hope you can help stop them."

"We hope so, too," you say as you and Edward leave the store.

Turn to page 10.

A small group of Indians holds a conference with Slickrock in a nearby shelter. When they come out, they ask you and Edward to join them. The eldest man speaks. "We are direct descendants of the Anasazi. If you wish to learn their history, you must make a very large commitment to them. You will have to join our group for one year, during which time you will not be able to let anyone know where you are or what you are doing. In effect, you will disappear."

A full year is a long time to be gone without letting your friends and family know where you are, although it would be a wonderful opportunity.

If you choose to join the Indians, turn to page 106.

If you decide that you can't just disappear on your friends and family, turn to page 21.

The closest telephone is at Bullfrog Marina, about two miles down the lake. You have to stop these men from blowing up the dam. Cautiously, you and Edward paddle toward the marina, following the canyon walls that serve as banks for the man-made lake you are on.

Once at the marina, you contact Larry "Skipper" Younghorn, who is in charge of the Lake Powell water police. Strange as your story is, you're surprised that he doesn't believe you.

"But, Mr. Younghorn, we heard them! It's true, they're really going to do it," you say, trying to make him take you seriously. After much talk, Skipper finally assigns two deputies to go and check out your story. At the last minute, he decides to go along himself.

The police boat, a twenty-two-foot Boston Whaler, skims the lake at over thirty-five knots. In no time at all you reach the camp where the men are. Skipper shines his light on them and yells over his loudspeaker, "Police. Remain where you are. We're coming ashore."

Turn to page 113.

"Slickrock," you ask, "when will we reach the first of the Anasazi sites that have been raided?"

"If we make good time today, we'll be able to reach the site by early tomorrow morning," he answers. "But you never can tell what we will run into on this river."

At the end of the day, you pull the rafts out of the river and set up camp on a grassy hill, the canyon walls soaring above you. Soon you set a large campfire roaring, and over dinner the talk turns to the Anasazi. You marvel at the power and the energy of these mysterious people now long gone. As you settle in for sleep under the stars, you imagine the souls and the spirits of the Indians as they seem to hover in the canyons, still and vibrant. During the night you drift into restless dreams.

Turn to page 111.

After one day of discussion, you and Edward are certain that the opportunity is too great to pass up. Your choice was a difficult one, but it is met with a wonderful surprise—Slickrock, he reveals to you, is one of them—he is an Anasazi descendant!

It is now time for your initiation. Slickrock tells you that you must first take part in a very sacred ritual that will last for ten days. It is a cleansing ritual that involves dances and talks with the elders.

Afterward, Slickrock comes to speak with you and Edward. "We are about to show you our most valued secret. I want to warn you that it may come as quite a shock to you." Slickrock leads you to the foot of a slender waterfall that slices down from a canyon wall.

"Climb as high as you can," he says, handing you a rope that leads into the waterfall.

After giving the rope a good strong tug, you and Edward begin your climb. When you are about thirty feet above the ground, you hear a voice coming from inside the waterfall. "Come here, to your left," it says.

"Who are you?" you ask. "Where are you? All I see is water."

Suddenly a hand reaches out and guides you into a cave hidden within the waterfall.

"Follow this cave. Here, take these lights."

Turn to page 14.

The first site is only about a mile into the canyon. It was easy pickings for the thieves, you realize.

Once you reach the site of the raid, your heart sinks. The damage is far worse than you had expected. Walking among the ruins, you can hardly tell that this was ever an Anasazi dwelling. The ground is pitted with digging, and the walls of the houses have been knocked down.

Picking through a pile of rubble, Edward finds a leather folder bearing the name Elk Mountain Mining Co. "Hey! Look at this! I think I've found our first clue! There are maps inside the folder of all the Anasazi ruins in this area."

"Where is this Elk Mountain Mining Company?" you ask.

"I don't know," Edward replies. "Let's go back and see if we can find anything in the state records."

"Maybe we should stay in the canyons and continue searching," you reply.

"Let's flip a coin," Edward suggests. Your guide, Phillip Moss, says nothing. His eyes roam the silent canyon walls. You can't tell what he's thinking.

"Heads we go back. Tails we stay," Edward says, tossing the coin into the air. "You call it."

Heads, turn to page 34.

Tails, turn to page 22.

Watching carefully through the binoculars, you see the men pull into a small area that was once probably a vast canyon.

"We can paddle to that cave over there," Edward says, pointing to the distant shore. "They won't see us."

The lake is calm, and you have no trouble crossing. With the canoe hidden onshore, you and Edward climb up the steep wall to the mesa. "We can watch from here, no problem," you tell Edward as you look down at the water far below you. The men are making camp on a small plateau.

"We'll wait until dark, then we'll make our move," you say.

The day is long and hot. The water looks inviting, but swimming is out. You can't risk being seen. Finally night descends, and the air begins to cool.

Together you and Edward launch the canoe and push off into the darkness. Your paddles make plopping sounds in the calm, black lake. You aim for the roaring fire that marks the men's campsite. Their voices carry out across the water to you.

"Did you hear that?" Edward asks you. You nod. "They want to blow up Glen Canyon dam! Who are these people?"

"They'll kill hundreds of people. Quick, let's get the police," you say.

Turn to page 103.

Slickrock leads you to a simple shelter that will serve as your home for the next year. Once there, he tells you the ways of the valley—Anasazi do not own anything here because they can have anything they wish from the land that they harvest. There is also no crime because everyone is happy with life in the valley. Those who are not happy are free to move to the outside world; however, they are sworn never to reveal the secret of the Anasazi. Those who have tried to lead others back have magically lost their way, unable to find the valley.

When you ask the Anasazi if they have any idea who is stealing the pottery from the ruins of their ancestors, Slickrock answers, "Many years ago, when the Aztecs attacked us, we left directions to this valley hidden in secret writing on the pottery. We are fearful that the wrong people might discover this writing and find our valley. So it has been the Anasazi themselves who were stealing the pottery!"

Turn to page 73.

"Wake up. Wake up. We've got a long day ahead of us. Let's get going," Slickrock yells, banging a spoon against a pot.

After some bacon, eggs, and thick coffee, you are back on the river. As you were warned, the river is much rougher today. The rafts bounce up and down on small rapids, and large waves crash against the bows, sending sheets of water over everyone.

"Here we are," Slickrock yells as he pulls his raft over to the side of the river. "The ruins are just a short hike up that canyon over there."

Slickrock's idea of a short hike turns out to be three miles up steep canyon walls in double time. You finally reach the ruins and slump down to rest against the rocks. You are shocked to see the damage that has been done to these old buildings. All the shelters have been knocked down, and the earth around them has been dug up. Everyone is amazed at the damage except Mr. Chinaua; he has seen some of the other sites that the thieves have raided.

After a few hours of searching, the only clue any of you find is an empty pack of cigarettes. Disappointed and sickened at the needless destruction, you return to your rafts and the river.

Turn to page 20.

112

The ritual continues all night until dawn. Finally everyone lays out bedrolls and goes to sleep. Fatigue overwhelms you, Edward, and Slickrock, and the three of you retreat to a safe distance.

When you waken, you can see the Indians walking in a long line into an adjoining canyon. You join the end of the line, trying to look inconspicuous.

Suddenly you see a large rattlesnake strike a small boy, who falls to the ground screaming in front of the crowd. Acting purely upon impulse, you run to the boy and grab a large rock that you smash over the rattlesnake. The snake dies quickly, twisting and turning in the sand. With a knife you make a small cut over the wound left by the snake on the boy's leg and suction the poison out of his cut with the rubber cap from your water bottle. He lies frightened, wide-eyed, watching your every move.

Turn to page 13.

Two deputies search the camp. They find the explosive and quickly arrest the four men. Apparently they are members of an organization that calls itself the Glen Canyon Liberation Front. After a court hearing they are all convicted on charges of conspiracy to create malicious damage and injury.

You and Edward are highly commended for your work; but you still haven't figured out who's been pilfering from the Anasazi ruins. Unfortunately, it turns out you have followed the wrong men out of the cave. When you do return, Josephine, Phillip, and Mary are nowhere to be found. It looks like it's going to be a long summer.

The End

ABOUT THE AUTHOR

ABOUT THE AUTHOR

RAMSEY MONTGOMERY is the author of *The Mona Lisa is Missing* in the Choose Your Own Adventure series. A graduate of the Green Mountain Valley School, Ramsey studied in England for a year, and went to the University of Vermont. He completed a ninety-day winter mountaineering course at NOLS (National Outdoor Leadership School) in the Wind River range of Wyoming. Summers find Ramsey house painting and writing Choose Your Own Adventure books on Nantucket Island. In the winter he can be found skiing the Hobacks at Jackson Hole.

ABOUT THE ILLUSTRATOR

LESLIE MORRILL is a designer and illustrator whose work has won him numerous awards. He has illustrated over thirty books for children, including the Bantam Classic edition of *The Wind in the Willows*. Mr. Morrill has illustrated many books in the Skylark Choose Your Own Adventure series, including *Home in Time for Christmas, You See the Future, Stranded!,* and *You Can Make A Difference.* He has also illustrated *The First Olympics, Mystery of the Sacred Stones, The Perfect Planet, Hurricane!, Inca Gold, Stock Car Champion,* and *Alien, Go Home!* in the Choose Your Own Adventure series. Mr. Morrill also illustrated both Super Adventure books, *Journey to the Year 3000* and *Danger Zones.*

ENTER THE YEAR 2015...
TRIO: Rebels in the New World
An exciting new futuristic series of books

Matt Sampson...Mimla Caceras...David Hasgard. Three teenagers fighting for the life they once knew. Code Name: TRIO.

After decades of international war and destruction, the United States has splintered into two battling territories. Trio must fight to protect the free and democratic Turtalia from conquest by the totalitarian Doradans — and their evil dicator, Arthur Gladstone!

Follow TRIO's exciting, action-packed adventures on all their daring missions.

☐ 28347-2	TRAITORS FROM WITHIN #1	$2.95/3.50
☐ 28382-0	CROSSING ENEMY LINES #2	$2.95/3.50
☐ 28462-2	ALMOST LOST #3	$2.95/3.50
☐ 28486-X	THE HIDDEN EVIL #4	$2.95/3.50
☐ 28515-7	ESCAPE FROM CHINA #5	$2.95/3.50
☐ 28550-5	DEADLY ENCOUNTER #6	$2.95/3.50

Bantam Books, Dept. TO, 414 East Golf Road, Des Plaines, IL 60016

Please send me the items I have checked above. I am enclosing $_____ (please add $2.00 to cover postage and handling). Send check or money order, no cash or C.O.D.s please.

Mr/Ms _____

Address _____

City/State _____ Zip_____

TO-7/90

Please allow four to six weeks for delivery.
Prices and availability subject to change without notice.

CHOOSE YOUR OWN ADVENTURE ®

- ☐ 27227 THE PERFECT PLANET #80 .... $2.50
- ☐ 27277 TERROR IN AUSTRALIA #81 .... $2.50
- ☐ 27356 HURRICANE #82 .... $2.50
- ☐ 27533 TRACK OF THE BEAR #83 .... $2.50
- ☐ 27474 YOU ARE A MONSTER #84 .... $2.50
- ☐ 27415 INCA GOLD #85 .... $2.50
- ☐ 27595 KNIGHTS OF THE ROUND
           TABLE #86 .... $2.50
- ☐ 27651 EXILED TO EARTH #87 .... $2.50
- ☐ 27718 MASTER OF KUNG FU #88 .... $2.50
- ☐ 27770 SOUTH POLE SABOTAGE #89 .... $2.50
- ☐ 27854 MUTINY IN SPACE #90 .... $2.50
- ☐ 27913 YOU ARE A SUPERSTAR #91 .... $2.50
- ☐ 27968 RETURN OF THE NINJA #92 .... $2.50
- ☐ 28009 CAPTIVE #93 .... $2.50
- ☐ 28076 BLOOD ON/HANDLE #94 .... $2.75
- ☐ 28155 YOU ARE A GENIUS #95 .... $2.75
- ☐ 28294 STOCK CAR CHAMPION #96 .... $2.75
- ☐ 28440 THROUGH THE BLACK HOLE #97 .... $2.75
- ☐ 28351 YOU ARE A MILLIONAIRE #98 .... $2.75
- ☐ 28381 REVENGE OF THE
           RUSSIAN GHOST #99 .... $2.75
- ☐ 28316 THE WORST DAY OF YOUR LIFE #100 .... $2.75
- ☐ 28482 ALIEN GO HOME! #101 .... $2.75
- ☐ 28516 MASTER OF TAE KWON DO #102 .... $2.75
- ☐ 28554 GRAVE ROBBERS #103 .... $2.75

Bantam Books, Dept. AV6, 414 East Golf Road, Des Plaines, IL 60016

Please send me the items I have checked above. I am enclosing $_____
(please add $2.00 to cover postage and handling). Send check or money
order, no cash or C.O.D.s please.

Mr/Ms _____

Address _____

City/State_____ Zip_____

AV6–7/90

Please allow four to six weeks for delivery.
Prices and availability subject to change without notice.

CHOOSE YOUR OWN ADVENTURE ®

☐ 26983-6	**GHOST HUNTER #52**	$2.50
☐ 28176-3	**STATUE OF LIBERTY ADVENTURE #58**	$2.50
☐ 27694-8	**MYSTERY OF THE SECRET ROOM #63**	$2.50
☐ 27565-8	**SECRET OF THE NINJA #66**	$2.50
☐ 26669-1	**INVADERS OF THE PLANET EARTH #70**	$2.50
☐ 26723-X	**SPACE VAMPIRE #71**	$2.50
☐ 26724-8	**BRILLIANT DR. WOGAN #72**	$2.50
☐ 26725-6	**BEYOND THE GREAT WALL #73**	$2.50
☐ 26904-6	**LONG HORN TERRITORY #74**	$2.50
☐ 26887-2	**PLANET OF DRAGONS #75**	$2.50
☐ 27004-4	**MONA LISA IS MISSING #76**	$2.50
☐ 27063-X	**FIRST OLYMPICS #77**	$2.50
☐ 27123-7	**RETURN TO ATLANTIS #78**	$2.50
☐ 26950-X	**MYSTERY OF THE SACRED STONES #79**	$2.50

Bantam Books, Dept. AV, 414 East Golf Road, Des Plaines, IL 60016

Please send me the items I have checked above. I am enclosing $_____
(please add $2.00 to cover postage and handling). Send check or money
order, no cash or C.O.D.s please.

Mr/Ms _____

Address _____

City/State_____Zip_____

AV–2/90

Please allow four to six weeks for delivery.
Prices and availability subject to change without notice.

Choosy Kids Choose

CHOOSE YOUR OWN ADVENTURE ®

- ☐ 26157-6 JOURNEY TO THE YEAR 3000 Super Edition #1 — $2.95
- ☐ 26791-4 DANGER ZONES Super Edition #2 — $2.95
- ☐ 26965-5 THE CAVE OF TIME #1 — $2.75
- ☐ 27393-0 JOURNEY UNDER THE SEA #2 — $2.50
- ☐ 26593-8 DANGER IN THE DESERT #3 — $2.50
- ☐ 27453-8 SPACE AND BEYOND #4 — $2.50
- ☐ 27419-8 THE CURSE OF THE HAUNTED MANSION #5 — $2.50
- ☐ 23182-0 SPY TRAP #6 — $2.50
- ☐ 23185-5 MESSAGE FROM SPACE #7 — $2.50
- ☐ 26213-0 DEADWOOD CITY #8 — $2.50
- ☐ 23181-2 WHO KILLED HARLOWE THROMBEY? #9 — $2.50
- ☐ 25912-1 THE LOST JEWELS #10 — $2.50
- ☐ 27520-8 SPACE PATROL #22 — $2.50
- ☐ 27053-2 VAMPIRE EXPRESS #31 — $2.50

Bantam Books, Dept. AV8, 414 East Golf Road, Des Plaines, IL 60016

Please send me the items I have checked above. I am enclosing $_____ (please add $2.00 to cover postage and handling). Send check or money order, no cash or C.O.D.s please.

Mr/Ms _____

Address _____

City/State _____ Zip_____

AV8–2/90

Please allow four to six weeks for delivery.
Prices and availability subject to change without notice.